The Animals' Football Camp

by Clare De Marco and Trevor Dunton

W
FRANKLIN WATTS
LONDON•SYDNEY

First published in 2013 by
Franklin Watts
338 Euston Road
London
NW1 3BH

Franklin Watts Australia
Level 17/207 Kent Street
Sydney
NSW 2000

A CIP catalogue record for this book is available
from the British Library.

ISBN 978 1 4451 1610 5 (hbk)
ISBN 978 1 4451 1616 7 (pbk)

Series Editor: Jackie Hamley
Series Advisor: Catherine Glavina
Series Designer: Peter Scoulding

Printed in China

Franklin Watts is a divison of
Hachette Children's Books,
an Hachette UK company.
www.hachette.co.uk

Jungle United were training for The Animal World Cup.

3

The team worked hard at a special camp… except Lion.

"I don't need to train," he roared. "I'm already brilliant!"

The other animals were cross with him.

"We're a team!" they cried.

6

"We need to learn to play together!"

But Lion didn't listen.
He woke up late each
morning.

He dozed each afternoon.

Before long, it was time
for the first match against
Amazon Athletic.

The team played well…
except Lion.

He kept taking the ball off
on his own.

He kept trying to score,
but missing.

And he let Amazon Athletic score!

At half time, Meerkat
Manager took him off.

"You're supposed to be defending!" he shouted. "Hippo, you're on!"

Hippo gulped. He was
clumsy and slow.

But he did play well with
the team.

Hippo stopped Amazon
Athletic's star striker.

He passed the ball up to
Giraffe and Gazelle.

Soon Gazelle scored.

It was **1-1**.

23

Then Giraffe got a header
from Hippo's cross. GOAL!

The whistle blew.

"Well done, team!"
Meerkat Manager cried.

JUNGLE: 2
AMAZON: 1

Next day, everyone trained
hard for the next match.

And guess who trained
the hardest? Lion!

Puzzle 1

Put these pictures in the correct order.
Now tell the story in your own words.
How short can you make the story?

Puzzle 2

calm   angry

bossy

lazy   sleepy

modest

Choose the words which best describe
each character. Can you think of any
more? Pretend to be one of the characters!

Answers

Puzzle 1

The correct order is:

1d, 2f, 3e, 4c, 5b, 6a

Puzzle 2

Meerkat The correct words are angry, bossy.
The incorrect word is calm.

Lion The correct words are lazy, sleepy.
The incorrect word is modest.

For details of all our titles go to: www.franklinwatts.co.uk

*hardback